Briar Rose
and the
Golden Eggs

Diane Redfield Massie

Parents' Magazine Press/New York

Library of Congress Cataloging in Publication Data

Massie, Diane Redfield.
  Briar Rose and the Golden Eggs
  SUMMARY: A dissatisfied goose pretends to lay
golden eggs in hopes of receiving better treatment from
her farmer.
  [1. Fables] I. Title.
PZ8.2.M38Br   [E]   73-1249
ISBN 0-8193-0684-3; ISBN 0-8193-0685-1 (lib. bdg.)

For Zora Belle

BRIAR ROSE was a big white goose.
She lived with the chickens
in Farmer Bean's barnyard.

"Chickens," said Briar Rose,
"are bores. They don't know
a seed from a stone."

"Cluck cluck cluck," said the chickens,
pecking at stones in the dust.
"Can't you say anything but 'Cluck'?"
asked Briar Rose.
"What else is there to say?" said the
chickens.

"Suppertime!" called Farmer Bean, leaning
over the fence. He poured the supper into the
trough. It splattered over the chickens.
"Mash again!" sighed Briar Rose.
"Cluck cluck cluck," said the chickens.

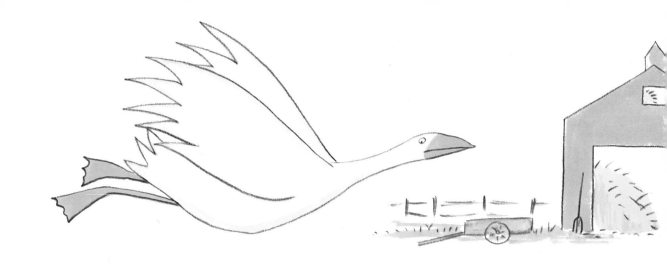

Briar Rose flew into the barn and settled herself
in the hay. "I'm tired of this simple
life," she said. "I'm tired of chickens. I'm tired
of mash. I'm tired of Farmer Bean's barnyard!"
She opened her fairytale book and slowly turned
the pages.

The Goose That Laid the Golden Eggs, read
Briar Rose aloud. *Once upon a time, there was a
goose who laid some golden eggs. Her master
was so pleased that he gave her a silken pillow for her
nest, and brought her delicacies to eat.*
"Now that's more like it!" said Briar Rose,
shutting the book with a bang. "Silk pillows and
good dinners."

She sat thinking in her nest that night long after the chickens had gone to sleep.

"Cluck cluck cluck," said the chickens in their dreams.

The next morning, Briar Rose found three
round stones behind the barn. She painted them
shiny gold. "I'll put them in my nest,"
she said. "Clever me!"

"MIRACLE!" shouted Farmer Bean, when he saw the golden eggs. "MIRACLE! MIRACLE!"

He ran and got Mrs. Bean.

"GOLDEN EGGS?" said Mrs. Bean.
"IMAGINE THAT!"
"WE'RE RICH!" cried Farmer Bean,
dancing around the barn.

They made Briar Rose a nest of silk pillows
in the best chair in the parlor.
"Nothing's too good," they said, "for a goose
who lays golden eggs."

Mrs. Bean took her shopping basket
and hurried off to town.

"You'll soon have delicacies
to eat," said Farmer Bean.

He took his feed bucket and
poured the mash outside
for the chickens.

"Cluck cluck cluck," said the chickens.
"Where's Briar Rose?"

"Here I am," said Briar Rose, looking
out the window, "inside where I belong.
My nest is a silken pillow and I shall have
delicacies to eat."
"Delicacies?" said the chickens. "What're
those?"
"The opposite of mash," yawned Briar Rose.
She shut the window.

Mrs. Bean came back from town.
"I have tea biscuits, tarts and
apricot twists. I hope Briar Rose
will eat them."

Briar Rose ate them one by one.
She sprinkled the crumbs on the
window sill.
The chickens stood quietly watching.

Knock! Knock! Knock!
"Someone's at the door,"
said Mrs. Bean.

"It's the whole town!"
said Farmer Bean, looking out. "What do they want?"

"We want to see the goose,"
they said, "the goose that lays
the golden eggs."
"Come in," said Farmer Bean.

The villagers came in, and they all looked at
Briar Rose. "You can tell she's a wonderful
goose," they said. "Where are the golden eggs?"

"In the breadbox for safekeeping," said Mrs. Bean.
They followed her into the kitchen.

"Solid gold!" said Farmer
Bean. "You can feel how
heavy they are."
"WOW!" said the villagers.

Now at the end of the line, unnoticed by everyone else, were two robbers. They carried a very large bag between them.

"Hurry," said one. "She's in the parlor!"

"Help!" cried Briar Rose, when she saw them.

"Into the bag with her," said the robbers. *SNATCH!*

They tied the bag at the top and hurried
out the door.
"Help! Help!" cried Briar Rose, inside the
bag, but no one heard her.

"WOW!" said the villagers, staring at the eggs.

"Cluck cluck cluck," said the chickens.

The robbers threw the bag in their truck and drove away.

The bag bounced up and down in back. "Help! Help!" cried Briar Rose.

At last the truck stopped, and
the robbers carried the bag inside.

"This is our hideout," they said,
undoing the string.
"Dear me!" cried Briar Rose.

"Now lay some golden eggs,"
said the robbers, "and you
won't end up in the stew."
"What stew?" asked Briar Rose.

"We haven't made it yet," said the robbers,
"but it's going to be *goose* stew, unless we get
some golden eggs."
"Golden eggs?" said Briar Rose, and she began
to cry.

"Put on the pot,"
said one of the
robbers, "and throw
in an onion or
two."

"Onions are good with goose," said the
other robber. He lit the fire under the pot.
"Heavens!" said Briar Rose.
"We'd better have some gold eggs by
suppertime," said the robbers, and they both
went outside.

"Oh dear!" sobbed Briar Rose. "If only
I were back with the chickens in Farmer Bean's
barnyard eating mash. What's to become
of me *now*?"
She looked at the pot steaming in the
fireplace, and covered her eyes with her wings.

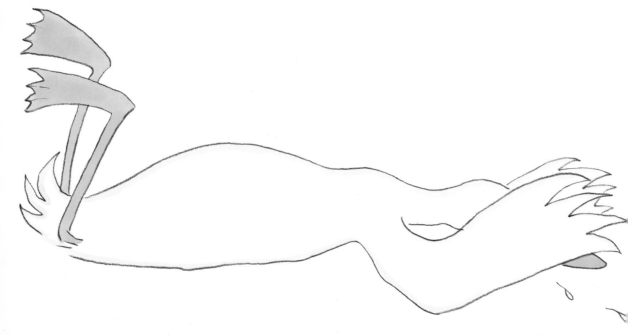

"It's suppertime," said the robbers,
stamping through the door. "Where are the
golden eggs?" And they grabbed up Briar Rose.
"NO EGGS?" said the robbers. "Then into
the pot with her. We're hungry!"

"HELP!"
shouted Briar Rose.

The door flew open with a
bang! And in came the police
with Farmer Bean behind them.

WHAP! WHOPP!
The police caught the robbers
and took them off to jail.

"There's Briar Rose!"
said Farmer Bean.
"Thank goodness she's
safe," said Mrs. Bean
from the old farm truck.

They put Briar Rose in back in the
hay. Mrs. Bean held the golden
eggs in her lap, and off they went
down the road toward home.

The sky was dark, and on the way it began
to rain.
Pitta patta pitta patta pitta patta, came
the rain.
"It's wet back here!" said Briar Rose.

The farm truck stopped in Farmer Bean's
yard.
"We're home!" said Farmer Bean.
"Everything is soaking wet," said Mrs. Bean.
They looked at the golden eggs.

"GOOD HEAVENS!" they shouted. "WHAT'S
HAPPENED TO THE EGGS?"
The golden eggs were stones again.
The paint had all washed off.

Briar Rose hung her head and sighed.
"You naughty goose!" said Mrs. Bean.
"Into the barnyard with you," said Farmer
Bean sternly. He opened the gate and
let her in.

"There's Briar Rose!"
said the chickens.

"It's nice to be back,"
said Briar Rose. She
pecked at a piece of mash.

"Why aren't you in the parlor?" asked the chickens. "Parlors are bores," said Briar Rose, folding her wings.

The chickens nodded among themselves. "Cluck cluck cluck," they said.

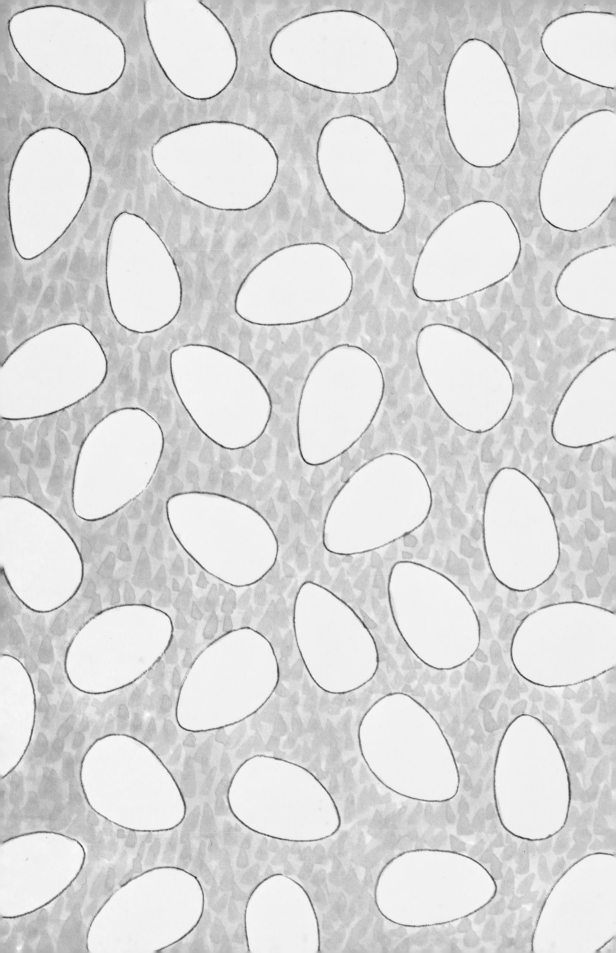